All the ingredients of classic fairy tale lore are contained in this adaptation of the original French tale, *L'Oiseau Bleu,* written by the Comtesse D'Aulnoy during the 17th century.

A romance—between the handsome Prince of the Blue Mountains and Princess Amber, daughter of an aged and failing King.

Many woeful trials—including a seven-year-long spell cast upon the Prince by the powerful fairy Soussio.

Evil and ugliness—embodied in the characters of the step-mother Queen and her daughter Zagzin who lock Amber high in a tower away from her Prince.

Good triumphs—the magician Magnadin who works his magic to save the Prince, and to achieve the universal happy ending.

*The Blue Bird*

# THE BLUE BIRD

*Adaptation by Erica Ducornet*
*of Mme. D'Aulnoy's old French tale*

---

Pictures by Erica Ducornet

ALFRED A. KNOPF    NEW YORK

••⊰[ *For* ]⊱••
Sarah and Diana Coover
and Elizabeth Haigh

*The Blue Bird*

# I

Once upon a time, in distant lands deep and green, there lived an aged King. His Queen was wise and beautiful and his daughter Amber was as warm as burnished gold. The King rejoiced in his gentle daughter, his Queen, and his thriving kingdom.

But one night the Queen died mysteriously, and the castle walls echoed with the sounds of mourning. Amber tried to comfort her father, yet she so resembled her mother that the very sight of her brought him more pain. Soon she was forbidden to visit him.

The King's sorrow was very, very deep and many feared he would take his life. One by one the storytellers came before him hoping to bring forgetfulness. Some were gay and wove ancient tales of love and magic. Some were grave and spoke of war, of frozen seas and glittering kingdoms. Many came but all failed to bring him cheer and a desire for life. The months changed, day slowly succeeded day. And still the King grieved.

One evening when the year was old and the sky was white with winter, a strange woman appeared at the castle. Her face was hidden beneath a black veil, and her body was draped in one hundred folds of velvet, soft and black. Only her slender white hands were visible.

She asked to be admitted to the Great Hall where the King sat with his court and once within she wept and wailed and tore her hair. When the King saw her,

he thought, *How like my despair is this woman's.* He beckoned her before him and said, "Woman, tell me your tale. And if it be sorrowful enough, perhaps I will find comfort in it."

"Only the weary can comfort the weary and the sorrowful comfort the sad," the dark woman replied. "Just as you, I am bereaved of a loved one and left with only a daughter to care for; just as yours, my sadness is deep. The world is filled with sorry souls, but few know our despair. Let us nourish our sadness day by day, hour by hour. Let us nourish this bitterness that it will flourish and not die!"

The King was drawn by the woman's dark words, and they talked and sorrowed together well into that night and into the many days and nights that followed. In this way the time passed until, grown weary of sadness, they came to speak of other things. At last, one evening, the dark lady let the veil fall from her face and looked upon the King with eyes deep and strange.

Soon thereafter, Amber was brought before her father in the Great Hall. The dark woman sat at her father's side, upon her mother's throne.

"This woman has eased my sorrow," said the King to his daughter. "I have asked her to be my Queen. Love her as your mother, and respect her word."

Amber bowed before her father and his bride, but though she tried to appear joyful, her heart was heavy and her mind was filled with foreboding.

Soon after the wedding, the Queen sent for her own daughter Zagzin. The girl had been brought up by her godmother, the powerful fairy Soussio, and she had grown to be both ugly and mean. The magpies scolded whenever Zagzin appeared at the window; the spotted toads leapt away when she walked in the gardens. When the Queen saw her daughter standing beside lovely Amber, her heart was jealous, and her mind stirred with evil.

In the months that followed, the Queen did all she could to turn her husband against his own daughter, saying that the girl was vain, foolish, and wicked. The death of Amber's mother had left the King weak in mind and spirit. Although he was fond of his daughter, he soon wearied of his new Queen's bitter tongue and proclaimed that both Princesses

should marry. Word was sent throughout the lands near and far that all who wished to court the Princesses should come before the King in the Great Hall.

One bright morning, a page dressed in silk and leather arrived at the palace to announce that the Prince of the Blue Mountains would seek the hand of one of the royal daughters. Immediately the Queen set her jewelers and embroiderers to work on gowns for Zagzin. That night, as Amber slept, the Queen crept into the girl's chamber and took away her beautiful gowns, gems, scarves, mantles, and jewel-studded slippers, leaving behind only a simple white dress.

When Amber found her clothing and jewels gone, she did not doubt that the Queen was responsible. For many months Amber had felt the woman's bitterness, and now she was truly angered, for she longed to see the Prince of the Blue Mountains. She had heard that his lands were vast, and his cities rich, teeming with men of all colors and customs. Yet the Prince had never sent armies to do battle, nor had he bid magicians to do evil. It was said that he was like a young tree in strength and in beauty, and that all who saw him wished to be his friend.

Amber ran quickly to the garden and picked green ivy and white lilies. These she spun into her hair and wove about her waist. Then wearing the simple white dress the Queen had left behind, she went to the Great Hall to await the coming of the Prince of the Blue Mountains.

Hiding behind a statue, so as not to be seen by the Queen, she watched the Prince enter. Proudly he stood before the King. The Great Hall, gleaming with gold and the fingers of ten thousand candles and humming with voices, became still. When the old King stepped down from his throne to greet the young suitor, the Prince smiled and Amber saw that his look was as gentle as it was proud.

But when the Prince saw the Queen approaching, nudging Zagzin before her, his face hardened. Zagzin's gown was of green silk embroidered with diamonds and yellow pearls, trimmed with an enormous yellow lace collar. Her wimple was green and gold, as were her slippers. *She looks like an enchanted toad,* the Prince thought, *all green and yellow, with diamonds and pearls instead of warts.*

He soon became impatient with Zagzin's chatter

and asked, "Princess, do you not have a sister?"

"Stepsister!" corrected Zagzin, pointing at Amber. "There she is, hiding because she is such a fool!"

At the harsh words, Amber blushed and became so beautiful, so very beautiful that the Prince, bowing deeply before her, said, "Fair child! Are you an elvin Queen? Your beauty is lovelier than the world!"

Hearing this, the Queen quickly spoke out. "Amber is already vain. Do not flatter her!"

But the young Prince was wise. He saw the Queen's envy. After asking the King's leave to walk with the lovely daughter through the royal gardens, he took Amber's hand as they left the Great Hall together.

That night, the Queen had Amber seized and carried to the topmost room of a high and deserted tower. Then she went before the King and told him that his daughter had fallen ill suddenly, and that she must not be disturbed, not even by His Majesty. By this lie the wicked Queen planned to keep Amber from the Prince without arousing the King's suspicion.

"She will stay in that dark tower," muttered the Queen to Zagzin, "until the Prince asks *you* to be his bride."

When morning came, the Prince wished to speak with Amber, but the Queen said that the King's daughter had no interest in anyone but herself. Nevertheless, the Prince asked for Amber again and again, so that at last the Queen had to answer him. "Sire," she said, "the girl is very ill and no one is permitted to see her."

Deeply troubled, the Prince at last retired to his chamber. There, in the guise of a friendly page, one of the Queen's spies awaited him. The Prince, unaware of the page's true loyalties, spoke to him openly of his love for the Princess and of his despair at being unable to see her.

Then, to his delight, the page told him that his sister was a servant to Princess Amber and that perhaps they could arrange a meeting without the Queen's knowledge. "But I beg you," said the page, "say nothing of this to anyone. If the Queen knows that I have helped you, she will surely throw me into the dungeon and leave me to perish." The Prince agreed to the plan, and the treacherous page went directly to the Queen.

While Amber wept in the cold tower and the

Prince waited impatiently for the page's return, the Queen prepared Zagzin for the part she was to play that night.

The page was ordered back to the Prince with news that a meeting had been arranged and that Amber would be waiting for him this night at a small, low window overlooking the garden.

The night was dark, without moon or star. And thus the Prince was fooled. Standing before the window, he said to Zagzin all that was meant for Amber. He begged her to share his love, his crown, and his realm. And he gave her his golden ring.

When the Princess replied, her voice was not soft and lovely as the Prince remembered and her speech lacked the elegance and charm that had so delighted him the day before. But he thought to himself, *The Princess must be terrified of the Queen and so fearful of discovery that she is not herself.* He did not leave until Zagzin promised to meet him again the following night.

The next night the Prince came for Amber in a chariot drawn by flying frogs. The chariot was a gift from a magician, and the wonderful frogs had a map of the universe in their heads and could fly to any distance in a single night.

His bride appeared before the Prince wrapped from head to foot in a purple mantle. Over her face she wore a veil, and she concealed her hands beneath the folds of her long skirts. When the Prince asked her where she wished to be wed, she replied quickly, "Take me to my godmother, the fairy Soussio!"

Flying high into the moonless night, they soon reached the fairy's castle. Made by enchantment and strange to behold, its towers soared into the sky as if in search of the moon that did not shine that night; its thousand windows flamed in the black sky. The chariot stopped before the great gates. The Prince and Zagzin quickly entered a hall so brightly lit that the Prince would surely have seen his mistake if Zagzin had not been so artfully veiled. Saying that she wished to speak to her godmother alone, Zagzin hurried from the hall.

Soussio greeted Zagzin warmly and said with surprise, "You have come with the Prince of the Blue Mountains!"

Then Zagzin told her everything that had happened, adding, "And so he has given me his word and his ring, and I wish to be married tonight. You must arrange it, Soussio."

"I have great powers, Zagzin," she said, "but love is also a powerful spell and the Prince's love for your stepsister is great and strong."

Now the castle walls were made of crystal, and as Zagzin spoke with Soussio, she removed her veil and mantle. Through the walls the Prince suddenly saw the ugly girl. As if turned to stone, he stood, his heart bitter.

Soussio led Zagzin toward him, and she met the Prince's eyes with eyes just as cold. Now the hall seemed made of ice. When Soussio spoke, her words bit into the Prince's heart like frost. "Here is the one to whom you have promised fidelity and love. All will be ready for the wedding within the hour. Welcome to my castle, and let us rejoice!"

"You must think me a fool!" cried the Prince. "I have promised Zagzin nothing!"

Soussio smiled and holding out Zagzin's hand with the ring said, "Is this not a promise?"

"A promise taken by trickery does not bind. Noth-

ing can force my love. Nor my word. You are using your Power in hate and not in love. Already I have stayed too long!"

"Stay, Your Majesty!" cried Soussio in a voice harsh and chilling.

The Prince's feet were as if nailed to the ground.

Then Soussio pointed a sharp finger at him and angrily cried, "*Adonai El Zaboath!* I conjure thee!" She clapped her hands, and laughing, she said, "Go proud Prince! *Fly* fool! Fly for seven years. This shall be my spell."

As she spoke, the Prince saw his arms melt into wings and his feet turn into shining black claws. His clothes fell from him, and his slender body was covered with gleaming blue feathers. His eyes shone black as the deepest sea, and a crown of white feathers adorned his head.

With a cry he flew from Soussio's castle, far from her icy and barren lands until at last he came to a deep forest, and there, perched on an ancient cypress tree, he wept.

# II

The Queen had been expecting her daughter to return from Soussio's castle in great splendor, preceded
by musicians and clowns, magicians and courtiers, and
followed by wedding gifts set on the backs of camels,
elephants, and gleaming white ponies. But when Zag-

zin arrived, she was weeping crossly, accompanied only by her godmother, Soussio. When the Queen learned the truth, her fury was terrible to behold.

"Amber shall suffer for this!" she vowed. "She will curse the day she set eyes on the Prince."

When Zagzin had recovered what few wits she had, the Queen dressed her in a gown of spun silver and set a crown of pearls and diamonds on her head. She summoned the daughters of the kingdom's richest barons and instructed them to hold Zagzin's train, and then led her up the thousand steps to Amber's prison.

Amber was amazed to see her stepsister so richly arrayed and the Queen, delighting in her cruel game, said: "My daughter has come to show you her wedding gifts. The Prince of the Blue Mountains has taken her for his adored bride. You can see that he has given her his ring and gifts of great richness."

Before Amber's astonished eyes, the Queen unrolled yards of rich brocades woven of gold and silver thread; velvet cloaks of purple, blue, and vermilion; lace as delicate as the spider's web; precious gems, and ribbons folded into birds of paradise and set in great baskets of spun gold, startling to behold.

As Zagzin touched these things, the golden ring flashed, and its sparks pierced Amber's heart. She could not know that these gifts had been produced by Soussio's magic. At last, weak with sorrow, she begged the Queen take the gifts and depart.

Once alone, Amber sank to the cold floor. For many hours she lay still without thought or hope. Finally she slept, but her sleep was troubled by strange dreams. She saw castles built of ice and trees bearing swords instead of fruit. She dreamed that she walked many miles, until, rising before her was a great white mountain that shone in the moonlight. Again and again she saw the wicked face of the Queen, and she shivered in her sleep.

The Queen relished Amber's torment. She told the King that his daughter was still very ill and would have to remain in the tower. Perhaps, had he been less wretched himself, the King would have insisted upon seeing his daughter. The sorrow of his beloved Queen's death had returned to him, and the new Queen's torments now devoured his heart and his mind. Day after day he sat upon his throne, his eyes vacant and staring blindly. He never spoke and rarely ate. When the Queen, to secure full power over Amber, told him that his daughter had at last died, he said nothing though his eyes glistened.

All this time, the Blue Bird had been drawing closer to the castle. He had flown one thousand miles over cold mountains and immense icy wastes. Across barren and terrible lands, he followed the sun, and the stars guided him. Then with the dawn he came to the castle.

He flew from window to window hoping to catch sight of Amber. When he did not see her, he feared that she was in a windowless room, or that if she lived she had been taken away, and then he would never find her.

At last he saw the tower and quickly flew to the high window. There he discovered his beloved Amber sleeping. In his excitement he beat upon the window with his wings. The Princess awoke.

Amber saw the beautiful bird at her window, and for the first time since her imprisonment she smiled. Carefully, she opened the window. The Blue Bird

alighted gently on her wrist and cried, "My love! I have found you at last!"

"A bird with speech is truly magical!" Amber marveled, but then she frowned and added, "Has Zagzin sent you? Oh, I can bear her torments no longer!"

At this the bird's eyes glistened with tears.

"Please, forgive me!" Amber cried. "You cannot possibly have come from Zagzin or the Queen. But why do you come?"

And so the Blue Bird made himself known to Amber. He told her of Zagzin's treachery and of Soussio's terrible spell. He explained why Zagzin wore the golden ring.

As for the gifts, the Prince said, "Trinkets of magic! Illusions made by Soussio from paper and glass beads. I will bring you gifts far more marvelous. And we shall be joyful, my love, despite our enemies. This I promise!"

All too soon night came, and the Blue Bird took wing. He flew deep into the sky until he came to his own lands. There, entering his castle by an open window, he took earrings fashioned of diamonds, so perfect and brilliant that they were unique in the world.

He returned to Amber with the earrings the next night. She scolded him for having made such a dangerous and long journey. "I care only for your love," she said. "All night I feared for your life. Who will save you from the hunters or the eagle? And who will save you from the great storms in the Blue Mountains and the wild gales on the sea?"

But the Blue Bird told her that his wings were strong, and could carry him far above the great storms. "And I have other wonderful things to bring you, Amber! Books bound in leather and gold, flowers made of gems, music boxes of ivory, porcelain, and crystal. I will bring you these things so that your hours will be full and quickly passing, and so that my memory will live in everything you touch."

The next night, the Blue Bird brought two bracelets, each carved from an emerald. Their color was like a young forest in spring, like the southern sea. And he brought her a clock so small it was nestled in a pearl!

Amber laughed. "I have no need for a timepiece! When you are not here, the hours are without end, and when you are with me, they pass like a dream."

Each day when the sun came up, the Blue Bird flew to the center of a certain tree where he nourished himself on its fruit. Often he sang, and his beautiful voice astonished animals and hunters alike, who stopped to listen and wonder. Soon, it was said that the woods were enchanted, and men in their fear dared not enter. And so the Blue Bird's hiding place was safe.

Two years passed and each day the Blue Bird brought Amber something beautiful. He invented countless tales of wonder—tales of forgotten things and of things to come, and tales of his own far kingdom.

And still the wicked Queen could not find a husband for Zagzin. She had sent ambassadors to offer her daughter's hand to every Prince in the land, and each time the ambassadors were sent back with this reply: "Amber's hand we would have received with joy! But the very thought of Zagzin makes us grimace!"

The Queen was bitter indeed. *So! Imprisonment is not enough,* she thought. *Amber's arrogance is not con-*

*tained by stone! It seems that she has sent secret emissaries who gossip against my daughter and myself!*

Late one night she and Zagzin went to the tower to scold and question the Princess.

Amber, dressed in gems, her magnificent hair shining with precious stones and streaming over her shoulders, had been sitting at the window with the Blue Bird, singing softly. Her room was filled with flowers, and on the floor were set tiny cups, smoking with fine incense. Amber's voice was pure and clear as spring rain. When her song was over, she and the Blue Bird began to speak together.

At the sound of their voices, the Queen burst in upon them.

"Traitors!" she shouted, expecting to find Amber with a conspirator.

The Blue Bird quickly took flight. All three watched as he drifted away above the forest.

Filled with hate, the Queen turned to Amber. How beautiful Amber was! Her dress was studded with jewels and rare metals that glowed like fire. "Where did you get these gems?" demanded the Queen.

Amber was silent and the Queen raged. "This tower

is mine. Everything in it is mine. Zagzin! Strip this thief of her stolen jewels!"

Zagzin tore at her stepsister's clothing, and where she ripped off bracelets and rings, there were left traces of blood.

Meanwhile, the Queen had begun to search the room. Overturning the straw mattress, she discovered rows of glistening pearls both black and white, diamonds, rubies, opals, sapphires, and stones even rarer than these. She ordered Zagzin to gather these things into her skirts.

"Insolent girl!" said the Queen to Amber. "Do not think for a moment that your conspiracy will go unpunished. As long as your fate is in my hands, you will not see your Prince again."

Zagzin had pinned many of the precious ornaments on her gown, knowing it would give Amber pain to see her wearing the Prince's gifts. Now she turned to her stepsister and said, "These jewels are mine, as your life is my mother's. She will keep you here as long as she wishes. And I will keep these pretty things. Do not think your father will come to your defense. He believes that you are dead."

After that, the prison door was double locked and guards were posted all around the tower. Night and day watchmen walked in the woods with orders to discover the Blue Bird's hiding place. A full month passed, but finally came a moonless night and Amber could call the Blue Bird without risk of his being discovered. Softly she sang:

> *Blue Bird! Blue as the mountains high!*
> *Blue Bird! Blue as the oceans lie!*
> *Amber awaits you! Quickly fly!*

Joyfully the Blue Bird came to her, and they spoke until the first signs of dawn.

The next night was also without a moon. Amber called again:

> *Blue Bird! Blue as the heaven's eye.*
> *Blue Bird! Blue as the northern sky!*
> *Amber awaits you! Quickly fly!*

And again the Blue Bird came, and the night passed as it had before.

But on the third night the sky was full of stars, and

when Amber called, a watchman saw the Blue Bird leaving his hiding place.

The watchman ran to tell the Queen who rewarded him richly for she was very pleased. At last she held the Prince's fate in her hands. She bid Soussio to hang the branches of the tree with sickles and knives, with hooks and swords, blades and shears. When the Blue Bird returned to the tree before dawn, his wings were cut and torn. In twenty places his body was pierced and hurt. And he fell, broken and dying to the ground.

The following night Amber called out again and again, but only the silence answered her. How vast the sky way! How empty. Why had the Blue Bird not come? Deeply afraid she waited at the open window through the night. It was very cold, and the wind blew, but she felt nothing.

# III

To the north, the Blue Mountains stood like great pointed pyramids; to the south, they took the form of wonderful animals. They were crusted with green forests and flowers—blueweed, gayfeather, and wood sorrel. Ancient trees housed small and fearless creatures in their sprawling roots. The peaks of the mountains were white with the snow of many great storms, and they shone by sun and moonlight.

These lands belonged to the Prince, and here lived Magnadin, an ancient enchanter and the Prince's friend. It was by his hand that the frog chariot, the enchanter's Spring's Eve gift to the Prince, had been wrought.

This same chariot had waited for some time outside Soussio's castle, but when the Prince had not appeared, it had returned to its first master, Magnadin, who seeing that it was empty feared for his friend's life and set out in search of him.

In two years, Magnadin explored the world's every corner eight times. At last, weary and about to give up hope, he passed through the Enchanted Forest. Walking with his head bowed, he suddenly saw a spot of color on the ground—a color so luminous in the darkness that he knew it to be of the Black Art. He knelt down and there found a strange bird, torn and dying.

With precious herbs and words of ancient power, the enchanter worked a cure. At dawn when the world stirred, the Blue Bird opened eyes clear and new with life. But the enchanter's astonishment was great when the bird knew him and said, "Magnadin! You have brought life to your friend, the Prince of the Blue Mountains! Take me far from this evil place. We have much to do, and I must remain prisoner to this form for five years more. The powerful Soussio wills it."

As they soared to the Blue Mountains Magnadin said, "Five years is very long. Already, your people have been without a sovereign for two years. When the chariot returned without you, I knew I must set out. Your subjects think you are dead, and men have come from the hills to destroy and pillage your lands. The people believe the Fates have turned against them, and so it seems."

"But what are we to do?" cried the Prince. "No land will be ruled by a sovereign in feathers!"

"I know Soussio well," Magnadin answered. "We have often fought, but each year we feast together in the Great Forest of Smihr when the mistletoe is ready to be gathered. I will take you to the Blue Mountains and leave you with Sewnsleave, my apprentice, while

I visit Soussio. Perhaps with cunning I can convince her to unweave the spell."

"There is one thing," said the Prince. "I will never marry her goddaughter, Zagzin. This she will ask and ask again."

"You are not like other men," said Magnadin. "You hold the fate of others in your hands. If marriage will save your kingdom, you must marry."

Magnadin left his King and flew to Soussio's icy realm. Through twelve days and twelve nights they talked. At last Soussio said, "I will agree if you will accept two conditions. I will give the Prince back his form, but I will take part of his mind. Until the penance is done, he shall remember nothing of his past.

"And secondly," Soussio continued, "He must marry Zagzin, my goddaughter."

Magnadin thought for some time, but at last he agreed. The people need a ruler—I cannot refuse." And he thought, *I will tell the Prince that a nagging wife can be quieted with rich food and expensive presents.*

"Done then!" cried Soussio. "Tonight I will unweave the magic, and in a few hours he will be as before, though his head be without mirror or echo."

When Magnadin returned to the Blue Mountains, he found that Soussio had spoken truly. Though the Prince was once more a man, his eyes were distant. He spoke seldom and smiled rarely. Still, there was great rejoicing throughout the kingdom to celebrate the return of the sovereign. The people danced in the streets and feasted on roasted meat and drained countless barrels of wine.

# IV

In the time that had passed, much had happened to Amber as well. Her father had died, for he was worn and very old. The people soon tired of their despotic Queen and they came to the castle, proclaiming the King's daughter as the rightful heir to the throne.

In the days of confusion, Zagzin fled to Soussio, but her wicked mother remained, thinking she could quiet the revolt. But the throng forced open the heavy castle gates, and when all was quiet again, the evil Queen was found crushed beneath her chamber door.

Amber was discovered in the tower. From there the people carried her to the throne with great joy and made her their ruler. She was loved by all and was so well cared for that in little time she was once again strong and well.

After having appointed the wisest men of the kingdom to rule during her absence, Amber took a small leather pouch of her most precious gems and went out into the world alone in search of the Blue Bird.

As Amber walked, the moon grew old countless times. She passed the marsh lands and the great moors where the warbler nests. At night she saw the fairy candles shine in the meadows, and by day the sala-manders and the little birds stayed with her. She

picked wood sorrel, groundsel, and mayweed. Like the animals, she lived by gathering berries and sweet roots and drinking from the clear streams. Gradually, she left the mire, the meadow, and the woodlands and came for the first time to the sea.

Amber thought the great ocean a work of magic, and she marveled at the sand—the strange creatures it concealed and the lovely shells scattered on its surface. She saw plants unlike any she knew—mangrove and eelgrass and the seaweed that curled out upon the beach like lazy snakes. The gulls kept her company, and the little plovers made her laugh. But when she watched the gulls soar high above the green water she wept.

For many months Amber followed the ocean's rim, until the winds grew bitter and forced her to turn inland. There ancient forests protected her from the snows, and she chose the old, crooked, half-hidden paths that ran far from men but ever to the Blue Mountains. And so she wandered, staying never longer than a night in one place, always in lands unfamiliar and made silent by the winter.

One morning she woke to the sounds of birds and

found to her surprise that an old, old woman was watching her.

"Good morrow, Grandmother!" Amber said, happy to see someone after so many lonely months.

As the old woman answered, Amber thought she heard a soft song.

> *Pretty child! Lonely one!*
> *Thou passeth before my eyes,*
> *Dwelleth inside my mind. I wonder*
> *What bringeth thee, has summoned thee?*
> *Wither goest thou and why?*
> *Lonely child! Pretty one!*
> *I follow thee, stranger in this land,*
> *And wonder! My mind hungers*
> *For thy tale. Gifts in hand*
> *I have for thee, if thou wilt answer willingly!*

Amber's eyes filled with tears, and she said, "Good woman, I search for one whom I love. He dwells in the Blue Mountains."

"Pretty one, why dost thou weep?"

"I weep for the time's passing," said Amber. "I weep because the Blue Mountains stand ever distant before me."

"That is but the work of Magnadin's magic—an appearance only," said the dame. "Soon thou wilt be upon them. But first tell me thy tale, for I know the ways of the world and so perhaps can help thee."

Amber told her all that had happened since she had first loved the Prince of the Blue Mountains. And to her astonishment, when she had finished her story and brushed away the tears, she looked up into the youthful face of a fairy dressed in green flowers and green gems. Sea vines were woven in her hair, and four white gulls stood at her feet.

"I am Gimgreen" the fairy said, "Mistress of the Sea. A long time I have followed thee."

Gimgreen told Amber all that had befallen her lover while they had been apart, for she was a powerful fairy and knew many hidden things.

"Thou hast but little time, Amber," she warned. "Thy lover is to marry Zagzin within seven days!"

Then she called to her gulls and said to Amber, "These are the gifts of which I spoke." And as she talked each gull dropped one small crystal ball at Amber's feet. "Use these only in time of need," said Gimgreen.

Then the fairy gave Amber a silver mare with a harness of pearls and cried:

*New moon!*
*Old moon!*
*Moon blind!*
*Bird's eye,*
*Fly, Mirror, Fly!*

The mare leapt across the brook with Amber clinging to her silver neck and galloped to the distant mountains, which loomed closer with each stride of the glittering hooves.

By nightfall the enchanted mare had brought Amber to the foot of the Ivory Mountain, gateway to the Blue Mountains. The Blue Mountains could not be entered until the Ivory Mountain was first conquered. And here the mare left Amber.

Amber soon found that the mountain's smooth ivory sides were impossible to climb. Again and again she slipped and fell. Then, remembering Gimgreen's words, she took one of the crystal balls and easily broke it in two. Inside she found twelve wonderfully fashioned golden hooks. She put the hooks on her

hands and feet, and with their aid she easily scaled the slippery mountain.

When she came to the summit and looked down, she saw to her confusion that the entire valley spread before her was one gleaming mirror. This valley had many names. Some called it the Valley of Fools, or Fool's Paradise. To others it was known as the Valley of Lies, and to still others the Mirror of Life, or the Mirror of Truth. All around the mirror's edge bent thousands of grimacing men and women, laughing, jeering, and sighing with pleasure. Each one saw himself reflected in that magic mirror as he longed to be. The old crone was young, the fat man slender, the bony spinster plump and pretty. For an instant Amber forgot her sorrow and laughed out loud at them. Everyone looked up, and seeing her about to cross the valley, they shouted as one, "Go back! Go back! You will shatter the mirror! You will scatter our dreams! Go back!"

Amber took another crystal ball and broke it. Out flew a magnificent griffin with a golden beak and a bridle of silver bells. Quickly he carried her high above the mirror and deep into the lands that lay beyond. When they came at last to the gates of the royal city, Amber embraced the beast and thanked him.

"Find the Chamber of Echoes!" the beast cried as he flew away.

Amber rubbed her face with dirt so as not to be recognized, wrapped her mantle closely about her, and entered the great city. She came to a busy street where merchants displayed their goods in wagons or little stalls that spilled out in all directions, making it difficult to pass. She passed the moneylenders and the jewelers with little piles of stones and gold dust set out on lacquered trays, and old wrinkled men in white robes stooping over potions of love and vermillion medicines and talismans of precious blue stone. There were stalls filled with objects of copper and brass, and she heard the *tap! tap! tap!* of the metal craftsmen's hammers as they worked in dark rooms above the dusty streets. She passed the fruit market and saw pyramids of fresh dates humming with flys and baskets of golden grapes that smelled like honey. The streets smelled of incense, of men and animals, of grilled lamb and strong tea. Amber had never before seen a city and she marveled at so many sights.

As she walked, she begged that someone lead her to the Prince's palace. But the merchants laughed at her and cried, "Dirty little fool! The Prince prepares for his wedding! He has no time for the likes of you!"

But at last an old beggar woman said, "I will take you, daughter. But for a price. Have you anything to give me for my trouble?"

"Yes," said Amber, "I will give you this." And she took a small ruby from her leather pouch.

The city seemed to stretch on endlessly, but at last they came to a great stone wall, and the old woman, pointing to the gates that opened onto a green plain said, "Cross the plain and the gardens, and you will be there. Give me my prize, child!"

Amber thanked her and gave her the ruby. Then she ran onto the plain spotted with tall cypress trees. In the distance she saw a magnificent palace surrounded by gardens.

As soon as she had reached the palace, she entered the great hall where many courtiers and merchants were coming and going. Finally the Prince entered the hall, followed by Zagzin.

Amber was deeply touched by the sight of the Prince. He was handsome beyond her dreams, and her heart was filled with love and longing. But when she looked at Zagzin, evil and uglier than before, her heart felt cold, and she remembered that the trial before her would be difficult.

She had little time left, so she ran after Zagzin calling, "Your Majesty! Your Majesty! Come see the pretty things I have for sale! Look here! Are these not rare?" And she showed her the two emerald bracelets that the Prince had given her. Bracelets that had been safely hidden from the wicked Queen.

"Ha!" exclaimed Zagzin. "These are worth mere pennies."

"They are worth much more," said Amber. "Ask the Prince their worth!"

Zagzin took the bracelets to the Prince, but to Amber's dismay his eyes remained dim, and he did not recognize his gifts of long ago. He knew their great value, however, so when Zagzin returned, she said, "I want them. What is their price?"

Amber replied, "Let me sleep this night in the Chamber of Echoes."

"Done, fool!" cried Zagzin, delighted to have the gems for so little.

The Chamber of Echoes was built beneath the Prince's own bedchamber and was made in such a way that the slightest sound within it could be heard in the room above. It had been built by the Prince's grandfather who had liked to fall asleep to the beating of hummingbird's wings but who would not have the birds themselves in the room with him. The hummingbirds had long ago been set free, and the room was now a storehouse for relics.

That night, Amber stayed in the Chamber of Echoes. With words she wove dreams and memories, images of the past, hoping that her words would prove stronger than Soussio's magic. But morning came, and she knew that she had failed.

Though Amber's words might well have broken the spell, they could never break the charm of belladonna. Ever since the Prince had lost his memory, he had been unable to sleep, and every night before retiring he took belladonna in the form of a carmine sugared heart.

The next day, Amber called after Zagzin once

again, "Majesty! Your Majesty! Come see what pretty things I have this day!" She broke open the third crystal ball, and out came a tiny green chariot, perfect in every detail. Its wheels were polished steel, and its seats were green leather. Inside sat six green mice dressed in lace and six green parrots dressed in yellow shirts. It was pulled by twelve purple rats, and a marionette in shining black boots cracked the whip and did wonderful tricks. Zagzin was delighted and clapped her awkward hands.

"Oh! What a splendid toy!" she cried. "I'll give you gold pennies for it!"

"No," said Amber. "I do not want gold. I want to sleep in the Chamber of Echoes."

Zagzin thought to herself, *The girl is very dim; this toy is worth a lake of gold,* and she agreed.

Once again, Amber spent the night hoping to give the Prince back his memory and make him whole. But when the sun came up, she knew that she had failed a second time.

"What shall I ever do?" she worried. "I have only one ball left from Gimgreen. And if I fail again to-night?"

She went again to sit in the great hall with the other merchants. As she brooded, a young page came to her and said, "Last night as I stood by the Prince's side, I heard your words of love. If you speak truly and are indeed the gentle Amber, then I, too, must speak truly. Each night the Prince is given belladonna to make him sleep. Nothing can awaken him until morning."

"Kind friend, do not give him the potion tonight," pleaded Amber, "and I will give you these rare jewels." The page looked at the sparkling gems and gave his word.

That afternoon Amber called after Zagzin again. "Majesty! Your Majesty! See what enchantments I have for you this day!"

Amber broke open the fourth and last crystal ball, and out came a freshly baked pie, still steaming, with six sparrows on it who sang new songs in six ancient languages and told fortunes and gave cures for the toothache and bad bones.

Zagzin cried, "For this, I will give you my sapphire ring!"

"No," replied Amber, "I want no gem. Only let

me sleep once more in the Chamber of Echoes!"

Since Zagzin was especially pleased with her prize she said, "Here, you may have the ring as well." It was one of the rings which Zagzin had taken from the tower, and Amber thought, *This must be a good omen.*

That night the lovely Amber stood once again in the Chamber of Echoes. As the hours passed, she wove a spell of words with love so deep and true that the evil charm was overcome and the Prince's memory was restored.

As he woke from the spell, he listened with wonder to the voice which told softly the story of his love for Amber and of her returned devotion. Quickly the Prince dressed and ran down the steps that led to the Chamber of Echoes, for the voice, he knew, came from there. He thrust open the door and there before him Amber stood, her hair free and her eyes glistening in the candlelight, her dress sparkling like the sun and the smile on her lips more precious, more lovely than a universe of stars.

They approached each other and embraced, and for a time they stood in silence and joy. Then there

came a knock upon the door, and Magnadin and Gimgreen entered.

"Your love has proven stronger than magic," said Magnadin. "Your lives are now your own. Soussio will never again harm you."

"But what of Zagzin?" asked Amber.

Gimgreen smiled and said, "If you look quickly out the window, perhaps you will see her before she flies away!"

The lovers turned to the window and saw a small ruffled owl slowly making its awkward way from branch to branch into the deep forest.

Amber and the Prince of the Blue Mountains celebrated their marriage and lived in great joy, their love increasing with the years passing. They ruled wisely, and their lands flourished. In time the palace gardens were filled with the laughter of their children. And so the story ends.

## About the Author

Erica Ducornet is especially fond of fairy tales. She discovered the original French version of *The Blue Bird* while reading a volume of fairy tales by Mme. D'Aulnoy.

Mrs. Ducornet, a 1964 graduate of Bard College, presently lives in Canada where her husband Guy teaches French literature at McMaster University. The Ducornets spend their summers in the Loire Valley with their young son. The author-illustrator has had a number of group and one-man shows both in this country and abroad. She recently illustrated a version of *Beauty and the Beast* by Mme. Leprince de Beaumont for Knopf.

*Text set in Bembo*
*Composed by Westcott & Thomson, Inc., Philadelphia, Pa.*
*Printed by Universal Lithographers, Inc., Cockeysville, Md.*
*Bound by L. H. Jenkins, Inc., Richmond, Va.*
*Typography by Jane Byers Bierhorst*